Dancing
with
Daddy

Willy Welch
illustrated by Liza Woodruff

WHISPERING COYOTE PRESS

Published by Whispering Coyote Press
300 Crescent Court, Suite 860, Dallas, TX 75201

Text was set in 16-point Tiffany Medium Italic.
Book production and design by *The Kids at Our House*
10 9 8 7 6 5 4 3 2 1
Printed in China

Library of Congress Cataloging–in–Publication Data

Welch, Willy.
Dancing with Daddy / written by Willy Welch ; illustrated by Liza Woodruff.
p.   cm.
Summary: Engaged in a joyous dance, a girl and her father leave the house
and cause animals and trees to join them in a celebration of life.
ISBN 1-58089-020-2
[1. Dance—Fiction.   2. Father and child—Fiction.   3. Animals—Fiction.
4. Trees—Fiction.   5. Stories in rhyme.]   I. Woodruff, Liza, ill.   II. Title.
PZ8.3.W44Dan   1999
[E]—dc21   98-50798
CIP
AC

To my darling daughter, Molly Bess
—"May you have this dance?"
—W.W.

For Grandaddy
—L.W.

It's Saturday evening.
The dishes are done.
The radio's playing an old, pretty song.

"Dance with me Daddy!
"Let's dance to this song!"
Soon I am grinning and singing along
as Daddy and I begin dancing.
Dancing like sillies
around and around.
We're singing and laughing and dancing.

I'm up in his arms
it's almost like flying,
swooping and soaring without even trying.
My ear on his shoulder—
my Dad is so strong—
it's tickly and buzzy as he sings along.
Dad smells like coffee and sweet aftershave.

We fly by my Mama
and give her a wave.
We blow her a kiss while we're waltzing away.
My Daddy and I are dancing.
Dancing like sillies
around and around.
We're singing and laughing and dancing.

We dance through the doorway
and onto the lawn
down past the fence post and
soon we are gone
up to the pasture, waltzing along,
where the cows are all
standing and chewing and staring
at Daddy and me and the dance we are sharing.

Then bowing politely,
with musical moos,
the cows are soon whirling
in great curlicues—
dancing like sillies
with Daddy and me,
mooing and laughing and dancing.

We dance past my hickory
who shivers us by,
flinging his branches to the star-frosted sky.
His dance is graceful,
a rustling leaf song.
It seems he is laughing
and dancing along
with me and my Daddy,
the three of us dancing.

We dance to the river
where the willows join in
like lovely old gentlemen
with wrinkly old skin,
bowing their bowers
and waggling their leaves.

They're singing and dancing
with Daddy and me.

We cross the bridge
and the flow of the stream
where the fish start to frolic
with Daddy and me.
The river is waving
and burbling a tune,
a shimmering dance
in duet with a loon!

Now the deer in the forest,
tails flashing white,
start dancing with rabbits
and squirrels in the night.
Then foxes and frogs
and flowers begin

and we giggle as
hedgehogs and fieldmice join in.

Soon the ants and the fireflies,
butterflies, too
are bouncing
and twinkling
and fluttering through.

Above us a birdy ballet passes by,
twittering tunes
in the musical sky.
The whole world is dancing!
So joyously!

To think it began
with my Daddy and me.
Dancing like sillies
around and around.

Singing and laughing and dancing.